The MANY SHADES OF *Love*

Written by
Constance Menzel Manthei

Illustrated by Carol Schwyn Johnson

*Dedicated to all the family and friends
of Grandma Constance who have come to love her,
even though we haven't met her... yet!*

Acknowledgments

Grandma Constance, you are our hero. Thank you for writing this delightful story for us way back in the 1950s! We look forward to meeting you in heaven!

All glory to God who brings people together in surprising ways to show us His many shades of love!

In 2021, Cousin Darwin Cone generously shared with Ruth this manuscript which he inherited from his mother, Christel Manthei Cone (daughter of Constance Menzel Manthei.)

In 2024, Ruth Manthei Wilkey (granddaughter of Constance) edited the manuscript for publication.

Cousin Carol Johnson crafted the illustrations from her imagination after reading the story.

Friend Renee Williams edited Ruth's edits and recruited her friend, Michelle Glush to design the cover and layout.

Here's hoping that our readers may enjoy many shades of love in their own journeys through life.

Table of Contents

Blooming Love

The breeze carried an aroma of fresh green leaves and spring flowers as college students poured through the doors of every building. Some were rushing to their dormitories while others sat on the steps, leisurely discussing their day's activities.

Dick Larson, a slender man of twenty-two years, hurried with long strides to overtake a trim-looking young lady who walked briskly in campus oxfords with books under her arm. A shock of his curly brown hair had the habit of falling over Dick's forehead, giving his pale face a boyish look. He arrived happily at her side and his friendly greeting brought a joyful smile to her fine, intelligent face.

"Miss Esther, I finally made the grade and met up with you. For over a week, I've been trying to catch you and missed every time."

She looked at him with serious blue-grey eyes. "Oh, I'm

so sorry. You know I enjoy seeing you, but I'm just so busy these days, like all those who graduate next week. Time goes so fast and there is always extra work to be done. May I ask where you are going and what you will be doing after the college closes for the summer?"

He answered, "I am not quite sure. I'll probably travel."

Esther was surprised! "Aren't you going home?"

"Oh, I never told you about my home in California? Mother died when I was twelve years old, and Father passed away two years ago. I have no brothers or sisters; no one with whom to share my troubles, no one to fight with!" He chuckled, but secretly, he envied her and wondered what it would be like to have a family to come home to like Esther did.

Esther Armond did not laugh. She looked pityingly at him. *The poor boy! It must be hard having no one to love.* Her heart went out to him.

They walked quietly side by side for a while. Then Esther said, "My mother doesn't feel able to travel, so my little sister will come here next week to watch me graduate."

"How nice," Dick replied. "Can I be of any help? I could drive you to the station in my car if you have no other arrangements made."

Esther was delighted. "No, I haven't made arrangements yet, and I gladly accept your offer. I'm not sure yet when Belinda will arrive. I expect to hear soon and will let you know." By that time, they were in front of Esther's dormitory.

"That will be fine," he replied.

With a friendly farewell, she ran quickly up the steps.

Dick slowly turned to walk away. He remembered meeting Esther for the first time at a party. What made her attractive to him was her beautiful hair made up in a Gretchen-style. Those long black braids winding around her delicate head fascinated him. She always looked neat and trim. He also knew she was a sincere, faithful Christian. He had watched her closely and realized that, in comparison, he himself was far from the mark. He had no Christian rearing. Religion was strange to him and not very interesting. But to please her, he sometimes accompanied her to church.

As he entered his room, he threw his books on his desk and said aloud, "That settles it. I'll meet Esther at church next Sunday. I hope we can get better acquainted before her pesky little sister arrives."

Esther hurried to her large room with three windows and four single-beds nicely made up. Two dressers and four chairs with small desks completed the furnishings. She felt comfortable here. She was well-liked by her roommates and was always kind and helpful whenever needed. Otherwise, she minded her own affairs.

Esther sat down at her desk and immediately wrote a short letter home. She begged her mother again to please let her sister, Belinda, come to her graduation. "And be sure to let me know what time she will arrive! Love, Esther." Then Esther hurried out to mail the letter and be back in time for supper.

In just two weeks, Esther would be on her way home! She enjoyed studying and was a good student, but she was

happy at the thought of returning to Petoskey. She hoped to secure a position as Home Economics teacher at the high school to be near her mother while Belinda attended college. Then Esther's thoughts ran to Dick Larson. She hoped he would visit their home so he could meet her mother. The prospect roused a happy feeling within her. Life was looking rosy and full of promise.

Esther didn't see Dick until Sunday, when he was waiting for her at the church door. Afterwards, they walked side by side to his car where he helped her into the seat. He turned toward her and smiled. "Now where do we go?"

"Home, of course!" She smiled back at him playfully.

"Now, see here!" he said pleadingly. "All week, I've looked forward to taking you out to dinner. You won't refuse me, will you? It's our last Sunday here at college."

Esther decided quickly. "I'd be delighted to go."

He took her to his favorite restaurant where they enjoyed a delightful dinner. Esther informed him that the train on which her sister was coming would arrive the next day on Monday at 5:00 p.m.

Dick then drove Esther out into the country where nature was in its prime. The meadows were lush with green grass. Flowers were blooming in full glory. He stopped the car so she could pick a big armful of daisies to take to her room. After several hours of driving, they headed back to her dorm and she thanked him for the delightful afternoon. He admired her as she stood facing him with her arms full of daisies. Such a sweet picture!

"I'm sure the pleasure was all mine," he said and he truly felt just that. "I'll be here tomorrow in time to take you to the station."

Esther clung to her flowers with one hand and with her other hand she waved goodbye as he drove off. She looked down at the daisies and thought how sweetly their little faces looked up at her! A shiver of joy ran through her body.

In her dorm, she arranged the flowers in two vases, one for each dresser. How they beautified the room and cheered her heart!

Chapter 2

Selfish Love

Monday afternoon, Esther struggled to concentrate on her work while the day slowly passed like any normal day. Thirty minutes before the train arrived, she was ready and waiting for Dick to take her to the station. He arrived on time just as he'd promised, and off they went, as happy as two children. They arrived and seated themselves on a bench to talk.

Dick asked her to describe her sister: "Does she look like you?"

"Oh no, not at all. We don't even look like sisters."

Just then the train chugged into the station. They rose to meet it and waited while it came to a stop and passengers stepped out. Esther turned to speak to Dick just as his eye caught sight of a beautiful young girl on the platform. The girl spied them too and came running to Esther, kissing her on the cheek, and for a while they just asked and answered questions.

Then Esther turned to Dick. "My sister, Belinda, meet Dick Larson."

Dick was speechless for a moment as he faced the most beautiful young lady of seventeen that he had ever seen. Belinda, a slender blond with laughing blue eyes, standing five feet and seven inches tall, held out her hand in friendly greeting.

"Mr. Larson, I know you from my sister's letters and I'm very glad to meet you."

Dick replied, "I'm surprised! I expected to see a little girl."

"Yes, Esther always calls me 'little sister,' but now I'm taller than she is. I did a lot of growing in the last two years."

Dick picked up the bags that the porter had set beside them and carried them to his car. He looked flustered. The girls followed him to the car where he opened the doors and helped them into their seats. Esther felt depressed but didn't know why. She couldn't explain the feeling even to herself. Dick and Belinda kept up the conversation while they drove, with Dick taking every opportunity to glance in the rearview mirror at her sister's sparkling blue eyes.

When they reached the dormitory, he carried Belinda's luggage to the door and said, "I hope to see you two girls soon and often this coming week." But his eyes were on Belinda.

She smiled at him sweetly and said, "How wonderful to come to a strange place and find such nice friends. Thank you for driving us here." Esther remained quiet. It was impossible for her to say a word. How could a person be so happy one day and so utterly depressed the next?

As they entered Esther's room, the other girls gave Belinda a warm welcome and offered to show her around. Belinda basked in the attention. She knew she was beautiful and found favor everywhere she looked.

The days that followed were rather hard on Esther. Not a minute did she see Dick alone—he always seemed to be with her sister! Her sister was enjoying herself immensely and completely unaware of Esther's feelings about Dick. A good many young men seemed interested in Belinda, but Dick had the days mapped out for her and managed to always be her escort.

One evening Belinda said, "Esther, don't you feel well? You are so quiet."

Esther answered, "I'm fine. I'm only tired from studying for exams. It seems you're getting along all right. I hardly ever see you in our room."

"Oh, I'm having a wonderful time! I'm so glad Mother let me come. You surely must have enjoyed college here."

Esther answered, "You forget that I came here for study and not for enjoyment. You don't get good marks by playing around."

Belinda puckered her lips. "Don't you think you take life too seriously?"

"Not at all, my dear sister. I'm afraid you take it too lightly."

"Esther, you forget that I'm not a baby anymore. What's wrong with having a good time? You surely are good at picking out nice boys, like Dick Larson."

By that time Esther was ready to cry and walked into the

bathroom so her younger sister would not see the tears. She was worried and felt hurt. *What made me ask Mother to send her here? She won't listen to me and I'm afraid she'll get her heart broken or worse.*

Belinda came in, put her arm around Esther's neck and kissed her. "You're not angry with me, are you? You know I love you." Belinda could be very sweet when she wanted to be.

Esther responded firmly, "No, I'm not angry, but tonight you need to stay in or I'll send you home. I'm responsible for you, and Mother would never let you go out like you do here."

"If it pleases you, I will stay," she replied and kissed Esther again.

Arm in arm they walked back into the room. Esther's dark-haired roommate, Rose, was singing *Home, Sweet Home*. They all called her "Roly-Poly" because of her short-rounded figure. Rose stopped singing and said, "My boyfriend and brother are coming tomorrow to drive me home. And Mother is preparing a nice party for me." Then she danced around the room, happy to be going home with her loved ones. The girls in Esther's room tried to get most of their packing done that evening, as they would drive home with their parents and friends right after the program, while Esther and Belinda had to stay overnight and wait for the morning train.

When the graduation ceremony ended, Esther felt tired, more of soul than of body. Belinda was nowhere in sight, so Esther headed to her room, where she expected to find

Belinda waiting for her. She was ready to relax on her bed before they headed out for supper. She had lost sight of her sister with so many people hugging and saying goodbye. As she entered the building, she met the house mother. "Do you happen to know if my sister is here, Mrs. Brown?"

"I didn't see her. She probably slipped past me. Did you enjoy the day, Esther?"

"Yes, I did, and I want to thank you for all the kindnesses you have shown me during my last school year."

Mrs. Brown smiled. "It surely wasn't hard to be nice to you as you are a very well-behaved girl, my dear."

Esther thanked her again and walked up the stairs. She opened the door and was greeted by a dark empty room. She snapped on the light. Not a sign of Belinda. Where was she? *Dick must have taken her somewhere again. Has he no regard for me? Doesn't he care if I worry about my sister? And they didn't even congratulate me!* She sat down to think and said aloud to herself, "I graduated. I am supposed to be happy, but I feel sad." A tear slipped out and she prayed for strength as she started to pack the rest of her things.

There still was this and that to be packed. Oh, yes, the picture of her mother on the dresser! She dared not forget. She reached out to take it and saw a letter addressed to her lying beside it. Surprised, she saw it was her sister's handwriting! Her heart felt as though it would stop beating. She slowly opened the letter.

"Dear Esther: When you read this, Dick and I will be on our way to California where his father left him a fine estate.

We were married this afternoon. Forgive me, sister dear, but I am so very happy. Kiss mother for me and I will write soon. My love to Mother and you. Belinda."

Esther was shocked. *How can I ever face Mother with this news? She will blame me! I was responsible for looking after Belinda.*

Tears blinded her as she walked to the bed, threw herself down and cried bitterly. The tears relieved her a bit and she decided that, come what may, she would tell her mother the truth. Sooner or later Mother would have to know.

Esther thought,
This is mother-love!
Always forgiving
the misbehavior
of a child.

CHAPTER THREE

Healing Love

After a long sleepless night, Esther boarded the early train for home. Mother met her at the depot with a huge smile on her face. Esther knew she'd been lonely for her girls and was thrilled to see her. Mother kissed Esther on the cheek. "My dear, you look ill. You must need a rest! And where is Belinda?"

Esther led her by the arm and said, "Mother, let's go home and then I'll tell you all about it. Belinda is well and happy, so don't worry. I had no breakfast and I'm very hungry."

"No breakfast. You poor child."

"Yes. I was waiting for your good cinnamon rolls and egg pancakes. I haven't had them for so long. Real home cooking—I've missed it so!"

Mother could not drive home fast enough to take care of her daughter. How she loved her two girls! As soon as she entered the house, she urged Esther to take off her coat and

hat. "I'll have breakfast ready in a hurry," and she rushed into the kitchen.

Soon the table was set and a delicious breakfast was ready. Mother could barely contain her excitement and concern. "Sit down, Esther. I'm so happy you're home! I want to hear all about your graduation. But first, tell me about your sister."

"Mother, let's wait until after breakfast. Then we can talk. Won't you sit and have a cup of coffee with me?"

"Yes, I think I will. I'm anxious to know what's happened with Belinda."

"I will tell you soon enough." Esther knew her mother's heart was not strong so she needed to break the news gently.

After breakfast, Esther put her arm around her mother and led her into the living room where they sat side-by-side on the davenport. Then she said, "Now, Mother, I will tell you all that happened from the beginning to the end."

Mother listened intently until Esther had finished all that needed to be said and then she remained silent for a while. Finally, she spoke. "Esther, you did all in your power to do. How could I blame you? I, myself, couldn't have stopped them. I must admit, it hurts me that Belinda ran off like that. I tried to teach her to respect her parents. I know I was weak and let her have her own way much of the time. I will pray and hope it will all turn out for the best."

Mother asked many questions about Dick Larson which Esther answered as well as she could. At last she said, "Oh, how I thank God that I still have you, my oldest daughter.

But that poor child! May God protect and guide her!"

Esther thought, *This is mother-love! Always forgiving the misbehavior of a child.* Her kind words made Esther feel as though a heavy burden was lifted from her shoulders. It was Dick's duty now to take care of Belinda.

Esther felt it was her duty to take care of Mother and bring sunshine into her aging days, which she would enjoy doing. She could look forward to enjoying summer vacation with Mother, thanking God for the great blessing of a cozy home with a loving mother in it.

Her first major accomplishment was to secure the position of Home Economics teacher at the high school. Mother was so pleased with her success that she bought Esther a nice , little coupe to drive to school. Then they spent the summer taking little trips together, seeing the beautiful lakes and woods of Northern Michigan. Belinda wrote short letters occasionally telling Mother not to worry as she was very happy.

School started in early September. Esther loved her work and it brought her contentment. She met old friends and made new ones, and eventually her heart healed, and her life became full and satisfying again. On many days, arriving home from school, Mother would be waiting with small surprises and the kind of home comforts that only love can give. Sunday afternoons, when the weather permitted, they drove out into the country to see the bright fall colors of the trees and bushes. Whole hillsides of sumac turned blood red with a green bush sprinkled here and there. So beautiful to

see—no painter could fully reproduce it. Both mother and daughter were happy and content.

Mother cared for the house with the help of a cleaning woman who came once a week. But there wasn't a day when she did not think or speak of Belinda. "If only they could live a little closer to home so I could see her once in a while," she would say. Her youngest daughter did not write often. Mother would have liked to have a letter at least every week.

Esther would say, "Mother, don't you know? No news is good news! I know my sister. She would soon write if life treated her too hard, and I'm sure Dick is doing all he can to make her happy."

Mrs. Armond was a good mother and she often wondered where she failed in rearing her youngest daughter. She forgot that one can rear twelve children and not one may be like the other in character or appearance. It would be impossible for such a mother with all that work to handle each child differently.

Mrs. Wheeler, her next-door neighbor, once said to her, "Mrs. Armond, a mother with a big family reminds me of a hen with a big flock of baby chicks. The hen tries hard to scratch up some food for them. At the same time, she needs to keep an eye on each one. Before she knows it, one peeps for help. Then she runs after a straggler to coax him back to the brood. Oh, how relaxed the mother hen looks when her little chicks are tired out and take a little afternoon nap under her wings. Then she herself gets a little hard-earned rest. The same is true of a good old-fashioned mother. When

one of her children goes astray, she wonders until her dying day, *"Where did I fail?"*

CHAPTER FOUR

Letters of Love

Christmas brought two nice long letters and presents from Dick and Belinda. Dick wrote that he adored his wife, and he hoped they carried no hard feelings against him for eloping with Belinda. He said, "We are very happy together and expect Junior in July of the coming year. Then we will try to come and visit the baby's Grandma and Aunt Esther."

Mother Armond was so happy! She pressed the letter to her bosom, walking the floor back and forth. "I can hardly wait until Esther gets home from school to hear this good news."

Winter passed and spring was back again. Little crocus flowers peeked through the still-cold ground to look around and let the sun shine on their pretty heads. How wonderful the world was after awakening from a death-like sleep through a harsh winter of ice and snow! *Just like the resurrection will be,* Mother thought. *Our eyes will be opened to a new life.*

School would be out in June, and Esther intended to stay home with Mother to enjoy another summer vacation. There would be a colorful flower garden to care for and fresh fruits and vegetables to be canned. Esther was ready to relax from teaching and do altogether different work through the summer. When Fall came, she would be rested, healthy and strong for another school year. Esther was pleased and content with her life. She was not like so many young girls her age who were never satisfied and wore themselves out grabbing for things they couldn't reach.

On a warm forenoon in late July, Mother and Esther were sitting in the kitchen cutting string beans for canning. Esther said, "If we keep up all this canning, we'll have enough food in the cellar to feed a small army!"

"Yes," Mother smiled, "Just think what we will save on the grocery bill the coming winter, and if it gets real icy out-of-doors, I won't even have to go outside. I'll just go down the cellar steps for a good nourishing meal."

"You're right." Esther replied. "And I really enjoy helping you. We have food that can't be found on any shelf in a store."

Just then the doorbell rang. Esther untied her apron to go to the door where she greeted a messenger boy with a telegram. She paid the boy and looked at the envelope. *It's from Dick, I'm sure!* She walked into the kitchen, waving the telegram. "I think we have a Grandma and an Auntie in the family. Here, Mother, you open it." She sat beside her mother so they could read the happy news together.

Mother's hands were shaking with excitement. Esther

smiled and waited patiently for her to open the telegram. They read it together. Esther's face turned white. Mother screamed, "No, oh no, it can't be!"

The message read, "Belinda dead. Come quick." They sat after the first reading as though paralyzed. It couldn't be! Healthy, lively Belinda…dead! Impossible! But there it was in plain harsh words. Dead!

Esther put her arm around her grief-stricken Mother. "The Lord gave you that child for a while, but now He has called her Home. I am sure she died a Christian. We are all only wanderers in this world, as you well know." She pressed her mother's head against her. "Cry, Mother, cry!" The tears finally came. Mother cried against the shoulder of her only remaining daughter. She had such a longing to look upon her younger daughter one more time but knew it wasn't meant to be. And it was much too far for her to travel for the funeral.

Esther knew she had to go at once. She called the station and was advised that a train would leave in two and one-half hours. She immediately packed her suitcase and asked Mrs. Wheeler to look after Mother in her absence. Before her heart could fully grasp the situation, she was at the station bidding farewell to her crying mother.

CHAPTER FIVE

Courageous Love

The trip was long and tiresome. When Esther finally arrived in Ventura, she hired a taxi that brought her to Dick Larson's address. She was surprised to see a large stucco home with a red-tiled roof, surrounded by palm trees, bright flowers and lush bushes.

She rang the doorbell and a servant opened the door. "May I see Mr. Larson? I am his sister-in-law."

The woman stepped aside and said in broken English, "Please come in, Miss." Then she led the way to the living room. "Please be seated and I will call Mr. Larson."

Esther was left alone. She looked about the homey room with a beautifully decorated fireplace and overstuffed chairs. How wonderful it would be if Belinda would waltz in and greet her! Instead, the door opened, and Dick entered the room looking haggard, as though he hadn't slept in days. She was shocked to see him looking so different from their

college days a scant year ago. He seemed to have aged many years and acted indifferent as he greeted her.

"It is good you are here. How is your mother?" Esther felt Dick was forcing himself to ask. She could see it really didn't matter to him… Nothing mattered anymore. She felt sorry for him.

"Mother is overcome with grief. May I see Belinda?"

"Yes, I'll take you."

"Tell me, Dick, how did it happen? And the baby didn't survive either?"

"She lives." He spat the words out hatefully.

Esther jumped up. "You say the baby lives? A little girl!" She almost screamed. "Where is the baby? Show her to me!"

"No." he answered. "Don't you see? It's her fault! That baby caused my wife's death!"

"Dick," Esther said, "don't be so unjust and blame the child. That's terrible."

"You may think so if you like." Then he added, "I never want to see it again!"

The anger rose within Esther. "So what will you do with the baby?" she asked hotly.

"I don't care… Give it away to whoever wants it."

"How dreadful—your own flesh and blood! All right. I'll take the baby as my own, but you must sign off your rights as father." Her eyes were blazing at him.

"Anything you like," he said quietly. "First, I'll take you to see Belinda."

Dick was a terrible disappointment to Esther! In her

bitterness against her brother-in-law, she did not understand that he was utterly lacking in faith and could not accept the guiding hand of God. Dick was used to running his own life according to his own will, which now failed him completely. And so, he was lost in hate and bitterness and blamed the innocent child.

They drove quietly to the funeral parlor. When she witnessed the stillness of her once-vibrant sister, Esther broke into tears. How good that Mother couldn't see her! Even death could not rob Belinda of her beauty. She was a beautiful sleeper, never to awaken until the final judgment day.

Dick was a broken man. Next, he drove Esther to the hospital to see the unclaimed baby, but he stayed in the car. "I'll wait for you here," he said.

Esther was eager to see Belinda's child. She found an elderly nurse who was very friendly and informed her that she was Mr. Larson's sister-in-law, Esther, and would like to see her niece. She stood outside the nursery while the nurse showed her the infant through the glass. Such a tiny little girl! The nurse tried to wake her up but her eyes stayed closed in sleep while she stretched her little arms and legs.

Esther loved her already. If only she could take that little human doll into her own arms and hold her! Esther knew she had a lot to learn about caring for a baby, but she was determined to do her best and she knew Mother would help her.

The nurse placed the tiny girl back into her little bed and joined Esther in the hallway. She told the nurse, "As soon

as possible after the funeral, I'll come back to take my little niece home."

"Where is your home?"

"I live in Northern Michigan."

"Oh dear, so far away in the cold North!"

Esther smiled, "The climate is wonderful. I would rather live there than any other place in the world. I'll give you my address, and someday, you may like to come to see our beautiful countryside."

Dick was silent as he drove her back to the house. When they walked in, he finally spoke. "You must be tired from the trip. Manda will show you to your room."

Esther followed Manda to a fine, large room. She looked around at the spacious bed covered with a heavy satin spread, the large chest of drawers with a picture of Mother displayed on an embroidered doily, and a dressing table with a full-view mirror. Two big windows afforded a view of the garden. Esther was still standing and looking about when Manda reappeared carrying a delicious-looking lunch on a tray.

She said in a motherly tone, "Miss Esther, you must be tired from your long journey. You will rest better after a little lunch. Please let me help you." Manda placed Esther's coat and hat in an adjoining closet and moved a chair in front of a cocktail table.

Esther did enjoy the food. She was hungrier than she had realized. Manda stayed and answered many questions. Between Manda and the nurse, Esther learned all she needed to know without bothering Dick with questions.

The funeral was private and quiet. Immediately afterward, Esther took care of the legal procedures to adopt the baby. Dick was indifferent and gave no help whatsoever, other than signing the papers and driving her to the store to buy clothes and diapers.

When they arrived at the hospital, the same friendly nurse greeted Esther and instructed her about the formula and feeding times. The baby was on a schedule, of course, which was all new to Esther. She would just have to do her best until she got home, where Mother could teach her everything she needed to know.

They traveled only during the daytime to make it easier for the baby. Esther had informed Mother of their estimated day of arrival and knew she would be counting the days, hours, and minutes until she could meet Belinda's child! It was hard to believe.

When the taxi stopped in front of the house, Mother rushed out as fast as her old legs could carry her. Esther placed the infant into her waiting arms, then helped the driver with the luggage. When she walked into the house, she saw the baby was lying on Mother's bed and Mother was bending over the little one with tears in her eyes. She turned to look at Esther and said: "Belinda's baby! My granddaughter! Belinda left her to us. May God bless her here in this home. From now on, my granddaughter will have the best of love and care."

The wee one slept while Mother and Esther sat in the living room, discussing all the happenings of the past weeks.

Finally, Esther said, "Mother, I adopted the baby in a hurry, but on the way home I had time to think. On Sunday, I'd like to have her baptized and give her the name Ruth Mary. She will have our last name, but I want her to call me Aunt Esther. Of course, she will call you Grandma. When she gets older, we can tell her all about her mother and father."

Mother agreed with the plan.

*How wonderful to love
and be loved by an innocent
child—somebody to depend
on her and make life
worthwhile.*

CHAPTER SIX

Motherly Love

ittle Ruth became the sunshine of the house. She was a very pretty child with her father's eyes and her mother's light hair. Grandma's whole life now circled around her granddaughter. She even gave up her Ladies' Aid Days so as not to leave the baby with someone else. Little Ruth was great company for them both, laughing and playing and bringing new life into the house.

Time went on and Ruth was now three years old. She was a very healthy child who dearly loved her Grandma and Aunt Esther. Then came the first dark cloud into her young life. One day, Esther came home from school and found her mother sitting in her big easy chair with her sewing in her lap, but her hands were still and she didn't lift her head. Little Ruth sat at her feet playing. She put her finger to her mouth, "Sh! Sh! Grandma sleeping, Aunt Esther." Esther stopped short. "Oh my God." She ran to the phone to call the doctor.

He arrived soon after, only to state the fact that Mother was gone.

How Esther missed her dear Mother! She had lost both her mother and only sister and would have felt so lonely if sweet Ruth had not come into her life. Her niece was such a comfort and blessing to her in her sorrow! She pressed Ruth's little body close to her. How wonderful to love and be loved by an innocent child—somebody to depend on her and make life worthwhile. She said over and over, "Oh my baby, my darling baby. We still have each other."

Esther hired a dependable Christian widow, Mrs. Barth, to stay with them, and all of her own spare time she devoted to Ruth so she wouldn't miss her Grandma too much. She patiently answered all the childish questions about when Grandma would come and play with her. As time passed on, the picture of Grandma faded more and more from Ruth's little mind and she started calling Mrs. Barth "Grandma," which pleased the widow greatly.

Two more years went by and Ruth started Kindergarten, taking her first steps into the outside world. Esther watched closely over her little one and monitored the influence other children had upon her. She always gave ample time to Ruth, so she wouldn't need to go to others for the answers to her questions. Esther had promised that to herself and she was determined to keep her promise.

One Saturday afternoon, as Esther was correcting school papers, a thunderstorm rolled in while Ruth was playing in the garden. Esther jumped up to call her inside but the little

one was already running into the house. Cuddling into her aunt's lap, she whispered, "Aunt Esther, the Lord is bowling again. He threw the ball so hard, I was afraid it would fall through the sky and knock me over. Auntie, do you think God was angry with me? You know, I dropped asleep before I finished my prayer last night, you remember?"

Esther pointed out of the window. "It's not about you, darling. You see the rain? The garden needs it, and the flowers will bloom lovelier than ever because of it. The storm is a blessing from the Lord. Don't be afraid, my dear."

"I'm not afraid when I am with you, Aunt Esther. May I sleep a while in your lap?"

"You may, for a little while." Aunt Esther smiled and whispered into her ear as she held her tightly. "My baby."

The doorbell rang. Esther carried the sleeping child into the adjoining bedroom where she laid her down carefully. As she quietly opened the door, she froze—spellbound. The man standing before her was Dick Larson.

"Esther, may I come in?" he asked.

"Certainly, do come in." she stammered. She led the way to the living room. He followed. "Please take a chair."

He looked around. "Where is your mother?"

"She passed away two years ago. Dick what brought you here, may I ask?"

"What brought me here? Loneliness. I've traveled all over the world. I guess I was trying to run away from myself. Before I go home and settle down to resume my work, I had to see you, Esther. I wronged Belinda's child. And mine.

The only excuse I have is that I was insane with grief and bitterness. Where is my child? May I see her?"

Esther said "I'm sorry, she's sleeping. If you would like to see her, tomorrow is Sunday and you can meet us at the church door. Ruth is *my* child by law, and I love her more than anything in this world. She brought so much sunshine to Mother and she is a blessing to me."

He answered, "I know. I have no rights as a father, but I wish you would let me help support her."

Esther said, "We don't need your help! Mother left this home to me. We live comfortably and are very happy, so there is nothing for you to do but to leave us alone. You've brought enough grief to this house already," she said bitterly.

He looked down and said, "You speak hard words, Esther. I know I deserve them, but I pray that the Lord doesn't judge me as harshly as you do." Then he got up to leave. "I will see you at the church tomorrow. Goodbye."

Esther walked to the door, opened it, and motioned for him to leave. She muttered to herself as she watched him walk to his car. "I was hard on him, but I can't… I can't part with my baby. She belongs to me now. Dick rejected the blessing Belinda left him in her child and now he suffers for it, as well he should. The only thing he will get from me is my pity, so I'll invite him for dinner tomorrow."

The following morning, Esther helped Mrs. Barth arrange the dinner table before she and Ruth left for church. Ruth looked like a little doll in her pretty blue dress with a matching hat. They lived just two blocks from the church

and, when the weather was suitable, they always walked, which gave them the double blessing of getting their outdoor exercise at the same time.

Dick was waiting at the church door with his eyes fixed on his child. What a lovely little girl she was! She had his eyes and Belinda's lovely hair. He wanted to take her in his arms but feared that Esther would object. He knew he had no right to touch her. Little Ruth paid no attention to the stranger who walked beside them into the church. She heard the organ playing and was eager to listen.

Esther felt uncomfortable and hoped nobody would notice that a man was sitting next to her. The pastor preached a good sermon and she only hoped that Dick was listening.

After church, Esther invited him for dinner and Dick accepted immediately, seeming glad to see more of them. Little Ruth was a shy child. She did not take well to strangers. It pleased him greatly when he coaxed a smile to her sweet face at the table. How happy that little smile from his daughter made him! Six years before, he could never have imagined it was possible.

Mrs. Barth served a delicious dinner. For two hours, Dick enjoyed the company of Esther and his child. He carried the hope of being invited to stay for the day but no such invitation was given. At mid-afternoon, he bid them both goodbye. He could see that Esther had picked up that which he threw away—a child's love. Oh, how he envied her now! He knew he had only himself to blame.

Christmas arrived a few months later, bringing lovely

presents to Ruth from her father. The first package she received was addressed specifically to Ruth Armond. Her little eyes opened wide and she looked at Aunt Esther. "Can I open it?" Esther nodded and helped her cut the tape. Ruth was thrilled to go treasure hunting and her aunt enjoyed watching her. Then Ruth handed her an envelope. "Look, Aunt Esther. This one has your name on it." Inside was a check for a considerable sum of money for Ruth with the plea not to reject it. That week, Esther started a savings account that her little girl could access when she turned twenty-one years of age. It would give her a nice start in life.

Esther often thanked God through the years for the way her life was unfolding—a lovely home with meaningful work and the privilege of raising this child. How wonderful to have a sweet, small person at home waiting for her, depending on her for love and care! What a thrill to have those soft arms around her neck and the child's sweet lips whispering, "Aunt Esther, I love you so hard it hurts!" Then Ruth would point to her tummy and Esther would shake her head and smile. "So your heart is where other people's stomachs are supposed to be?" Ruth would solve the problem by making a circle with her hand and saying, "All heart," as she looked up lovingly at her aunt.

When Ruth was nearly twelve years old, Mrs. Barth, who had become a second grandmother, developed a problem with her health and needed to go and live with her daughter. She arranged for her niece, Anna, to take her place. Anna was a delightful young lady of eighteen years. She settled

into their home nicely and did her work well.

As Ruth started high school, she and Aunt Esther walked to school together like mother and daughter, contented and happy. There was a profound understanding between them. One day, Ruth said, "Aunt Esther, we have to describe a good citizen in school today. What is your opinion?"

"Oh, my dear, that's easy. If a person was raised to fear and love God, he also would be a model citizen, obeying the law and being orderly. Don't you think so?"

"Yes, Auntie, I know you are right. It goes together. But if a person doesn't love and fear God, how would you make a good citizen out of him?"

"My dear, that would be a hard job—too hard for me," she replied.

Ruth said "Hmm, I wonder..."

Anna's boyfriend was a military flyer serving his country. Two years later, when he came home safe and sound, they all rejoiced. It didn't take long before they decided to get married. Anna had no home of her own, so Esther hosted their reception. It was a small but lovely wedding. Ruth had decorated the living room and dining room with beautiful fall flowers and enjoyed doing it immensely.

After Anna was gone, they decided not to replace her. They would do their own cooking and have a cleaning woman come in but once a week. "Auntie," Ruth beamed, "You know I love to cook, and I learned a lot from Anna. You will be surprised." And indeed she was! It worked out wonderfully.

The thought of Ruth growing up and leaving home one day made Esther feel sick inside. She could only hope it would not be for a long, long time. She knew that life gives and takes, as hard as that may be. One day Ruth would have her own home and family, but at least Esther had the satisfaction of knowing that love would always bind them together.

Yes, Ruth,
you've chosen wisely.
You have my blessing.
Now, go!
God be with you.

CHAPTER SEVEN

Love Letting Go

Ruth was in her last term of high school when Aunt Esther received an airmail letter from Dick Larson. He wrote that he was very ill and was scheduled for surgery in ten days.

"Please, Esther, I would like to see my daughter one more time before I undergo this life-threatening operation. Grant me that favor. I will carry all expenses. Let her come by plane."

Esther sat for a long time, pondering whether to let her go. Ruth was so close to graduation, and besides, she would need to travel alone since Esther couldn't leave her own students at this time of year. To think of her darling Ruth going away by herself was hard. Ruth would have to decide for herself. *Whatever she chooses to do will be all right with me,* she thought.

Ruth was preparing lunch when her aunt called to her. "I'll be right there." A few moments later, she came into the room asking, "What is it, Auntie?"

"A letter from your father. Read it." Esther watched Ruth's face as she read the letter. The young woman wrinkled her brow and then a tear slipped down her cheek. After she finished, she looked inquiringly at her aunt.

Esther reached out to touch her hand and spoke tenderly. "Ruth, I want you to decide for yourself what to do. You no longer are a child."

"Yes, Aunt Esther. I need some time to think it over. You know I am slow at making decisions. I'll tell you after lunch." They ate quietly, not as usual, and washed the dishes together. Then they went back to the living room.

Ruth put her arm around Esther and kissed her cheek. "Auntie, I've thought it over. If I stay here and Father dies, I will have a guilty conscience all my life for not caring enough to go when he asked me to come."

Her aunt answered, "Yes, Ruth, you're right. You've chosen wisely. You have my blessing. Now, go! God be with you. I will pray for you."

"Auntie, I'll come back as soon as possible!"

Donna loved to gaze at the stars
above and imagine they were windows
in heaven through which the angels looked
down to see what was going on below.
But she never imagined a sleeping
angel would fall down to earth
right in front of their ranch!

CHAPTER EIGHT

A Child's Love

Esther and Ruth made arrangements immediately for the trip to California. Anna's husband, Joe, offered to fly Ruth to the coast. He was a good pilot and Esther trusted him to get her niece safely to California. Then a telegram was sent to Ruth's father stating the time of her arrival.

When they arrived at the airstrip, Anna was waiting with her toddler and infant to see them off. Joe was warming up the motor. He jumped out of the plane to stow Ruth's suitcases and said goodbye to his wife and babies. Ruth kissed Esther and whispered, "I'll be back soon. Don't worry."

The plane roared down the runway and they were off into the air. Esther waved a last farewell. "May the Lord bless and keep her," she murmured. Then Esther spent the afternoon with Anna, not quite ready to go home to an empty house.

Ruth had no time to grieve their parting. She felt

keenly excited as the plane rose into the air, watching Joe at the controls, then looking down at the rapidly-changing landscape. The many lakes of Michigan shimmered like pearls scattered amidst the fields and forests. She enjoyed her first airplane ride immensely!

Joe landed a number of times to refuel the plane as they flew across the country. The way he landed the plane was marvelous, as easily and lightly as a dove would light on her nest. Joe loved to fly! He pointed out landmarks as they passed near Chicago and over farmland, then crossed the Mississippi River, to the Great Plains with the Rocky Mountains in the distance. Ruth was intensely interested in everything. They always stopped before dark to find a motel and enjoy a light supper.

On the third morning, they crossed over the colorful mesas of New Mexico and Joe was just telling Ruth that she would soon see the Grand Canyon when the engine missed slightly. Joe was alarmed. He knew there was no airport nearby. The motor sputtered more and more until he knew he had no choice but to land the plane. The landscape below looked rocky and mountainous. Finally Joe announced, "Ruth, we need to land while there is still a chance. Help me look for something fairly smooth."

"Where are we?" Ruth asked.

"Looks like Arizona," he replied.

Ruth was frightened and quietly prayed that God would protect them. Joe's whole attention was fixed on finding the most suitable place in the rocky, rolling valley. Suddenly

Ruth spotted a dry riverbed and Joe agreed that it looked like the safest spot to attempt a landing.

This time the plane did not land as lightly as a dove on her nest. No! The plane bounced and bumped, tipped to one side and screeched as the wing was noisily ripped off. That was the last thing Ruth remembered.

Joe felt intense pain in his left arm, but he was able to move the rest of his body. His eyes quickly sought out Ruth. She lay on the floor of the plane, her eyes closed. He breathed out a silent prayer. *Please don't let her be dead!* Then he bent over the quiet figure to see if her heart was beating. Thank God, it was! With difficulty, he wiggled his way out of the plane. Then, with his good arm, he pulled the unconscious Ruth close to the opening where he could remove her quickly in case a fire started. He turned about in a circle to survey the landscape when he heard a dog barking. Never did the bark of a dog sound so good to him! Now, if the dog would summon its master, there would soon be help. He turned in that direction and saw a cluster of ranch buildings about one-half mile away. From the holster at his side, he drew his revolver and shot three times into the air as an SOS. He feared to leave Ruth lest something might happen to her in his absence.

It so happened that the plane's landing did not go unnoticed. Young Pete, the chore boy at the ranch, had witnessed the scene. Whenever Pete heard the roar of a plane, he dropped whatever he was doing and gazed upward until it disappeared.

From the kitchen door of the ranch house, a woman called, "When will you bring the wood? I told you to fill the wood box!"

He shouted back, "A plane just landed. Somebody shot three times for help."

"Well, don't just stand there! Run to the corral. Call Cowboy Sam and Old Pike."

Pete ran, his feet barely touching the ground, waving his arms while he yelled at the two men. Finally, they were able to understand what the excited Pete had to report. They dropped their work immediately and rushed to the scene.

Joe saw the three men running toward him and felt such a relief. He needed help quickly for Ruth. How fortunate they were near a ranch!

The men worked fast, asking no questions. They carefully pulled the unconscious Ruth out of the plane and laid her on a smooth bit of riverbed sand. At the same time, they ordered young Pete to run back to the ranch. "Call the doctor and bring us a clean sheet!"

Joe was sure his arm was broken. As he gazed upon the quiet figure of Ruth, he felt sick to his stomach. How would he ever explain this to Esther? He knelt beside her to listen to her heart again. It was still beating. Thank God, she was alive!

When Pete returned, the men gently rolled Ruth onto the sheet as a makeshift stretcher and carried her up to the large ranch house, where they laid her on the living room davenport. Mary, the housekeeper, hurriedly brought cold water in a pan, dipped a towel in it, wrung it out slightly, and

placed it on Ruth's forehead, repeating it often. She whispered to her husband, Sam. "What a pretty young lady! It's as if an angel fell from heaven right in front of our door." Their little daughter Donna was standing beside her parents and heard the word "angel." Donna loved to gaze at the stars above and imagine they were windows in heaven through which the angels looked down to see what was going on below. But she never imagined a sleeping angel would fall down to earth right in front of their ranch! The thought filled her little heart to bursting. She stood as close as possible, peering at the angel's face and wondering what would happen next.

Shortly before the doctor arrived, they heard the sound of approaching hoofbeats. The owner of the ranch rode up to the hitching post and jumped down to tie up his horse. Art Collins was a tall, slender man with a lean, suntanned face. Young Pete was the first to tell him the news. Pete led the horse to the barn while a few long strides brought Art into the house.

Art strode quickly through the kitchen and into the living room where he welcomed Joe to his ranch. "I heard you crashed a plane."

Joe replied, "Not exactly. I'd call it a forced landing."

Art turned to Cowboy Sam. "Did you send for Doctor Welch?"

"Yes sir, he'll be here soon, I reckon."

Art walked over to the couch to look at the other passenger of the plane and was startled by the beauty of the sleeping maiden. Like Joe had done before, he knelt to feel her pulse

and listen for her breathing. The heart was beating steadily, and thankfully she was breathing regularly and deeply.

"I think she will be all right," he said to Joe.

"I hope so!" Joe then told Art all the details of the trip. He hadn't quite finished when the doctor arrived—a big, friendly man of about fifty years of age. Joe said "Please, Doctor, take care of Miss Armond first. I'm most worried about her."

The doctor quietly examined Ruth while Mary stood by to assist him. It was impossible to take one shoe off, so he gently cut it open with a sharp knife from the ankle to the toe. The ankle was already badly swollen. As he finished his examination, he straightened his tall form and said, "Except for a badly sprained ankle and a concussion, I think the young lady will be all right." He turned to Mary. "Keep putting cold compresses on her head and ankle too."

Next, the doctor stepped up to Joe. "Now we are going to look you over. Hmmm… a broken arm. Feels like a clean break. What about the rest of your body?"

"Doc, except for my arm, I think I'm all right; just a few bruises here and there."

"We will take care of that arm. Could be a lot worse. We're just glad you're both alive! Landing in a rocky riverbed is not so good."

Joe laughed. "As a rule, Doc, I don't land in such places."

Art looked at Ruth and caught himself wondering what color of eyes were hidden under those long curly lashes. Doctor Welch was still tending to Joe's arm when little

Donna called out, "Mama, the angel is waking up!" All that time Donna had watched Ruth so she would be right there when her angel opened her eyes. Art Collins did the same.

As Ruth's slowly awakened, she gazed around with surprise. Then she remembered: the plane… the sputtering… the riverbed. "Where is Joe?"

"I'm here, Miss Ruth, as good as ever. How are you feeling?"

She smiled, "Could be worse, I guess. I'm thankful you're alright!" Ruth was thinking of Anna, back home with two babies. Losing Joe would have brought such tragedy to their happy little family. She thanked God that He had spared Joe for their sakes. She laid her hand over her eyes, feeling tired and shaken.

Mary patted her hair, "You'll feel better soon, Miss."

Art was studying Ruth. She had the most beautiful blue eyes he had ever seen in his life. The thought struck him how breathtakingly beautiful they would be if filled with love. He was brought back to the present when Joe asked for the nearest hospital.

"Please stay here," Art said. "We have plenty of room. In fact, I insist you stay with us until you are well enough to travel. It would be hard for you right now. You will have the very best care here. You were dropped in front of my house for a reason and you are very welcome guests, I assure you." That was a long and convincing speech for Art.

The doctor helped him by agreeing. "Yes! You will recover well here at the ranch. I'll drive out every day to see you."

Joe accepted the kind invitation with gratitude because he detested hospitals, and Ruth simply blinked her sleepy eyes.

Despite his slender build, Art was strong and gently carried Ruth across the wide hall into a comfortable guest room, where Mary purred over her like a loving mother. Little Donna followed her angel as closely as a shadow.

"Is this little girl your daughter?" Ruth asked.

"Yes, she is, and she thinks you're an angel who fell from heaven."

"Oh, I hope I don't disappoint the little darling. I'm far from being an angel."

Ruth admired the comfortable, large bed and old-style Colonial furniture of her room. After a light lunch, Mary herded her little daughter out of the room so Ruth could rest.

Joe had a smaller room on the other side of the house and was made very comfortable. That evening the ranch hands came into his room to talk. He enjoyed their company and they enjoyed hearing his stories about flying. A hospital would have been a boresome place for Joe, and he knew it.

The following morning, Ruth asked Mary if she could send a message to her father and Aunt Esther. Mary answered, "I'll see the boss right away, and he'll take care of that."

Ruth was surprised and asked, "Don't you own the ranch?"

"No, no, Miss Ruth. I've been keeping house here for almost ten years. Mr. Art—the tall, handsome man who carried you to this room—he owns the ranch and he's a mighty fine man."

"Where is his wife?" Ruth asked. "I don't remember meeting her yet."

Mary laughed. "Mr. Art hasn't gotten that far yet. He's pretty picky when it comes to women. I'll go and call him to take care of your messages."

Soon afterwards, Mary returned with Art. When he asked politely if he might come in, the color rose in Ruth's face. She wasn't accustomed to the company of attractive, single men and felt embarrassed. She managed to nod her head in response to his question, looking to Mary for reassurance. Art was carrying paper and a pencil. When he pulled a chair next to her bed and sat down to write, Ruth immediately dictated the addresses and messages she needed to send.

"I shall take care of this at once, my lady. How are you feeling?"

"Much better, thank you."

"I'm very glad to hear that. Dr. Welch will be here soon." Having said that, Art rose and left the room.

Mary then asked Ruth if her little girl might come in for a while. "All I hear her talk about is you."

Ruth smiled. "I'd enjoy her company. Let your little daughter come in and I'll watch her play." Ruth's kind words won Mary's heart completely. She would have done anything for Miss Ruth after that... for a mother's heart beats for her children.

After Art left Ruth's room, he walked over to check on Joe, who already was becoming a good friend. "I came to see

if you would also like to send a message back home. Your wife would probably like to know if you're still alive. I'm going to town and will take your letter to the post office. Do you still have a lot of pain?"

Joe said "No, I'm getting better right along. How's Ruth?"

"She looks more rested today. I'll be sending the messages she gave me for her father and aunt, one west and one east—far apart."

"Yes," Joe said, "not only in distance but also in heart. Her aunt is a mighty fine woman, and so is Ruth. I don't know the old man at all. My wife worked two years for Miss Esther." Art would have liked to know more, but that was all Joe had to say, so Art left for town.

Ruth was busy worrying. *What will Aunt Esther say when she hears I'm staying in a single man's home?* When Mary arrived to ask if she needed anything, Ruth expressed her concern about a possible scandal.

"Why, my dear child, I'm the one taking care of you, not Mr. Art. You are as safe here as a baby cradled in her own mother's arms, so don't you worry about your aunt. There is no reason for it."

Ruth had no more time to think. The door quietly opened and in slipped little Donna. She smiled shyly at Ruth and came closer. Ruth encouraged her with a welcoming smile and saw that Donna carried a ragged doll in her arm.

Ruth asked her, "Did you come to play with me?"

"Yes," she said, "me and my doll."

Ruth sent Donna to ask her mother for a needle, thread

and pieces of bright fabric to make dresses for the doll. As they were sewing, she was answering questions and telling fairy tales to the little girl. Donna was so happy! Her mother was always busy and never had much time to spend with her.

Back in Michigan, Esther was alarmed to receive Ruth's telegram. She immediately sent a night letter back, saying that as soon as school closed, she would come to Arizona and travel with Ruth on the return trip by train. Esther also informed her to stay right where she was until she was able to travel without harm.

Three days after Ruth's telegram reached California, she received a message from her father's doctor saying that he had needed to perform the operation sooner than expected in an attempt to save her father's life, but that the surgery had seemed successful. Ruth was thankful and said a prayer for her father.

Art stopped every day at the post office to retrieve Ruth's mail and deliver the incoming letters to her in person. She looked forward to his visits and always greeted him with a friendly smile. He found a wheelchair in town and bought it, instructing Mary to serve dinner for Joe and Ruth in the dining room. Mary said, "I declare, that poor child will enjoy being out of bed and in the wheelchair. I will be happy to bring her into the dining room." And so it happened that Ruth was able to join Joe, Art and Dr. Welch for dinner that evening.

The doctor seemed quite relieved and jovial. "I see our young lady is progressing fast! And look at Joe here—he's ready to ride the ranch! Or maybe another plane, Joe?"

Joe laughed. "Doc, give me a little more time and I'll

show you the skies!" Joe was enjoying his forced vacation and Mary's wonderful cooking. As the days passed, they ate every dinner together in the dining room. Ruth lost her shyness more and more and began to feel quite at home.

Nobody could keep little Donna out of Ruth's room. One morning the door quietly opened and Donna peeked in to see if Ruth was awake. Then she slipped in, carrying a tiny puppy in her arms and set the little fellow in front of Ruth on the bed cover. She said proudly, "For you, Angel." Ruth had never seen such a tiny dog in her life, except in dime stores. It almost looked like a toy! She picked the little dog up, set him on her hand and laughed. Donna beamed with joy.

Then they heard scratching at the door. Ruth asked, "What is that noise?" Donna looked guilty. Before she could answer, her mother opened the door and in ran the mother dog. One leap brought her onto the bed. She grabbed her baby by the back of the neck and, just as fast as she could go while carrying her burden, she ran out of the door. Ruth was startled. She had never owned a dog and all this was new to her, so Mary explained the situation. Ruth was fascinated to learn that the mother dog had five more pups but she left them behind in order to rescue the sixth puppy from Donna and make sure no harm would befall her little one. It reminded Ruth of the story of the lost sheep in the Bible.

Joe came to see Ruth and was raving about Mary's good cooking. "I almost wish we could stay here for a while longer. I've gained so much weight that Anna won't recognize me when I get back home. I also had a letter from your aunt.

She's very thankful that we are with such good people. I guess Anna told her what I wrote to her."

Afternoons, Ruth would sit in the wheelchair next to Joe on the big, enclosed veranda where they could overlook the yard and see all the interesting things going on there. She saw the mother dog leading her six wobbling pups across the yard. What a cute sight! The mama took them to a shady spot where she lay down to rest with her litter. Over each other they tumbled, growling and snapping. One little fellow crawled onto his mother and nipped her ear. She bit him lightly on the leg and he squealed and backed away. Ruth realized that the mama dog was training her puppies and punishing them when necessary, just as all good mothers do. When Mary brought out a dish of table scraps for the chickens, the mother dog jumped up to see if there was anything good in it for her. She growled at the chickens to scare them away, but they didn't give up so easily. The cocky rooster pecked the dog hard on her nose. To a dog, the nose is a tender spot and she objected loudly, rushing back to her puppies. Then the rooster flapped his wings and crowed. He had won the battle and wanted the world to know it! Ruth and Joe laughed heartily. Joe slapped his knee and said: "This is such fun!"

For the pleasure of the guests, the ranch hands broke in horses within view of the veranda. To Ruth this proved to be very exciting entertainment, for she had never seen such a performance before except in the movies. These horses were partly trained, accustomed to bit and bridle.

Some horses never make good riding horses and will try at every opportunity to throw the rider. Two such animals were among the herd at Art Collins' ranch. The ranch hands decided to show Ruth and Joe the art of staying on the back of a bucking horse. Red, the foreman, was an excellent rider. He did his job well. He had the boys take off half of the gate bars and jumped the rest with the horse, about six feet high, never touching the bars. He loved horses and was a quiet, steady man, slow to anger—qualities that make a good horseman.

*One voice stood out
above the others—a beautiful
tenor voice. She would never
forget that voice nor the
wonderful singing in
the quiet night.*

CHAPTER NINE

A Gentleman's Love

After a few days, Ruth was beginning to think that there was nothing like ranch life, and Joe agreed with her.

Art joined them every day for lunch on the veranda. He was a perfect host, doing his utmost to please his guests—good Western hospitality—but most of all he wanted to see Ruth and be near her. What a difference there was between this sweet and beautiful maiden and the cigarette-smoking, hardened girls he met in town. He found himself sitting on the porch railing more and more, entertaining Ruth instead of riding the ranch, and Ruth lost more and more of her shyness, looking forward to his visits.

One day, Ruth received a letter from her father's nurse, stating that Mr. Larson was hoping she would soon be well enough to come to visit him. Ruth wasn't sure what to think. She had to ask the doctor and seriously evaluate whether she was ready for another journey.

With Mary's help, she discovered that she could step on her foot very lightly, but the pain was still quite intense. Doctor Welch decided that she should stay at least three more days and then she would be able to use her foot lightly with the aid of crutches.

Joe said, "Miss Ruth, I'll stay here with you until you are able to travel to see your father. After I see you off, I'll go home in the opposite direction."

"Thank you for your kindness, Joe, but you must be anxious to see Anna and the babies. You don't need to wait for me. You can leave any time you're ready."

"No, no, I promised your aunt I would take care of you."

In her last letter, Aunt Esther had asked for the name of the owner of the ranch so she could thank him and his wife. Ruth knew her aunt would be alarmed to learn that their host was a handsome, single man. Ruth confided in Joe. He laughed and said, "Well, child, we were rescued and very lucky to strike a place like this. If I had the knowledge to select a ranch to land in front of, I certainly would have picked this one! If your aunt knows how well Mary takes care of you and how we all look after you, she will be very satisfied, I am sure. As soon as I get home, I'll tell her all about it."

Joe spent a lot of his time with the cowboys and enjoyed their friendship. When he found out how well they sang and played different instruments, he encouraged them to play under Ruth's window at night, saying, "She'll never forget it the rest of her life."

"All right, we'll get the boss in on that and sing for her," the foreman said.

The following night when Ruth was just dozing off, she was suddenly awakened by the sound of men's voices under her window, accompanied by the strumming of a guitar and a melodious harmonica. It sounded just grand! One voice stood out above the others—a beautiful tenor voice. She would never forget that voice nor the wonderful singing in the quiet night.

Just then, Mary came in. "Honey, did they wake you up?"

"Oh, Mary, it was wonderful. I'll never forget it!" And long after they stopped singing, she lay awake, thinking of that very special serenade.

The next morning as Mary wheeled her in for breakfast, Joe said, "How did you like it?"

"Oh, it was grand. Did you hear it too?"

"I'll say I did. It was the finest singing I've heard in a long time."

After breakfast, while sitting on the veranda, Art wondered how he might fulfill every wish he thought he saw in Ruth's eyes. How he dreaded the day she would be leaving. He knew he loved her as he had never loved a woman in his life. He said to himself, *"And didn't God bring her right to my front door? She must have been meant for me."* Then he noticed that Ruth was playfully twirling a beautiful diamond ring on her finger. Before he could stop himself, he asked, "Is that an engagement ring?"

She smilingly looked up at him and said, "Yes, it is."

He felt the blood drain out of his face. The shock was so great that he was unable to move or say a word. Oh, how his heart hurt—an engagement ring!

Ruth was still quite naïve and didn't notice the paleness of his face. Finally, she said, "It was my mother's diamond. Father sent it to me on my seventeenth birthday. I like it because it was my mother's, and I decided to wear it to please my father when he sees me."

It took some time for Art to grasp the meaning of her words, and he breathed a huge sigh of relief. Then he pleaded, "Please tell me more about your parents." He was surprised to learn that she did not know either one of them. Now he also understood why she was not more concerned over her father's illness. He was a stranger to his lovely daughter. That poor man! Art felt sorry for him. "Your aunt must be a wonderful woman."

"Yes," Ruth answered. "She is! Everybody likes her, and I hope you will meet her someday."

"So do I," he replied, and he meant it.

When the doctor arrived that evening, Joe inquired if it would be safe for them to travel the next day. Doctor Welch said, "I think so. Mr. Art and I made the arrangements for Ruth's convenience. He will take you both to the city in his car. From there, the train will take Ruth straight to Ventura where Mr. Larson's car will be waiting to take her to his home. We've also arranged good connections east for you, Joe."

"Then we will be on our way early tomorrow morning."

Mary asked Ruth not to tell her little daughter that she

was leaving. "Donna will cry her eyes out!"

"No, I won't tell her," Ruth agreed. "I will disappear the way I came, and you can tell her that an angel never forgets her friends. I will send her a nice big doll to remember me by, so she will be happy. The little darling, I love her so." Mary's eyes grew misty with unwept tears. Ruth was everything she looked for in a young lady.

A beautiful sunrise greeted the travelers as they left the ranch amidst cowboys wishing them goodbye and good luck. Their perilous landing had resulted in meeting the best of friends, and it was hard to leave. Art had positioned Ruth carefully in the back seat with the men riding together in front as dictated by tradition.

They arrived in good time at the depot where passengers stood waiting to board the train. When the whistle blew, Art asked Ruth to put her arm around his neck. She gazed at him in surprise and he explained in a friendly manner, "It will be easier to lift you out of the car that way." She felt light and soft in his arms as he carried her. She looked back at Joe for a quick goodbye.

"Please give my love and greetings to Anna and Aunt Esther!" Joe assured him that he would do so, the moment he arrived.

Art carried Ruth up the steps into the train and carefully let her down, helping her get settled comfortably into the cushioned seat he had reserved for her. Unknown to Ruth, he had hired a nurse to watch over her on the trip. The middle-aged woman was already in the seat facing her and

greeted her kindly, winking at Art to assure him that she would keep his secret. She would take the next train back to Arizona after Ruth was safely on her way to her father's house.

Art bent down and whispered to Ruth, "May I write to you?"

"Please do! I want to hear all about the ranch and the people I've grown to care for, and please tell me how the little puppies are coming along."

"I will start training one for you, the finest of the bunch," he promised,

"Oh, I would like that. To have a little dog all my own would be splendid!"

The train whistle blew, signaling family and friends to leave the train. Art waited until the last minute, hating to part from her. He looked with love in his eyes at Ruth, kissed her hand, and whispered, "Goodbye, my angel." Ruth giggled shyly and for a moment their eyes locked. The whistle blew again as the train started moving, breaking the spell. Art turned away and rushed to the door, jumping deftly down the steps and onto the platform. He stood beside Joe, waving at her until the train had disappeared. Then Art turned to Joe and said, "Ten days ago, I would not have thought it possible that I could feel so lonely."

"Yes," Joe laughed, "That happens when you love a woman. You can feel lonesome in your own home when the one who owns your heart is absent."

Dick's face sobered.
Oh, I see. He's captured her
heart. I hope he is worthy of
having her. I'm afraid
I just found her only to
lose her again.

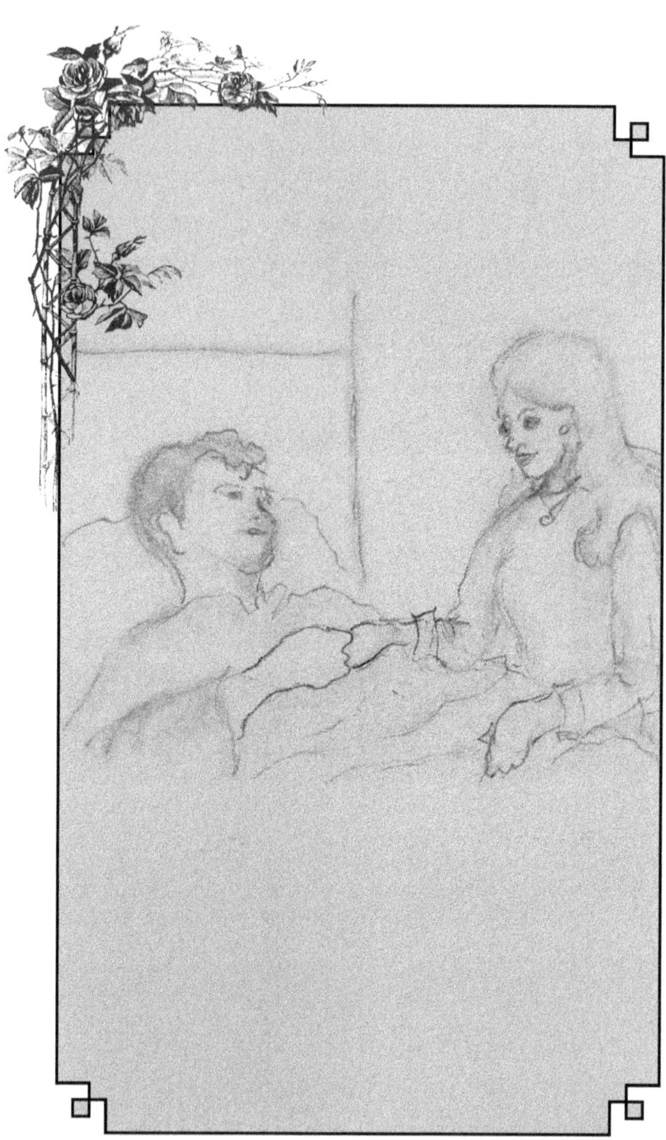

CHAPTER TEN

Father Love

A fter a pleasant trip, Ruth arrived at the Ventura depot where her father's driver was waiting for her. He helped her out of the train and into the car. Ruth had never seen palm trees before! Bright flowers bloomed everywhere she looked as they drove past front yards and roadsides.

She gasped when they rounded a bend, and the Pacific Ocean welcomed her with its glistening waves. It was almost more than she could take in!

Too soon they arrived at her father's house. Ruth was as surprised as Aunt Esther had been seventeen years before when she first saw the fine house and beautiful surroundings.

The driver offered his arm to help Ruth out of the car and stayed close behind her as she hobbled her way to the front door. He introduced her to Mr. and Mrs. Donovan who were keeping house for her father. They led Ruth into a cheerful room filled with fine furniture and fresh-cut

flowers. "Miss Ruth, we hope you feel at home and happy here," Mrs. Donovan said cheerfully.

Back in the kitchen, Mrs. Donovan said to her husband, "Jim, I like her. She's so polite and ladylike. I wish she were my daughter!"

"You have got the strangest wishes," Jim replied. "Why not wish for a million bucks? It means about the same thing. You won't get it. And if she were your own daughter," he continued, "how long would you have her? Some good-for-nothing man would take her away from you."

"Well," she laughed, "If you had a million bucks, how long would it last? You would spend it as fast as you got it, and it would soon be gone, I'm sure."

He left the kitchen. *No use arguing with women. They are unreasonable and always want the last word.* He went out and polished the car, expecting to drive it a lot with a young lady in the house. "I hope she will soon be on her feet so I can drive her around."

With Mrs. Donavan's help, Ruth soon walked fairly well. The next morning, she said, "I would like to see my father today. With your help," she added, "I can walk better now." That afternoon Ruth and the Donovans left for the hospital. She felt awkward about meeting her father. She wasn't quite sure how she should greet him. He still was a stranger whom she had met only once as a child and who sometimes sent her gifts.

Dick was sleeping when she entered his room. The Donovans said they would return in an hour to give her

privacy with her father and, as she looked down at his sunken face, pity arose in her heart. *He's my father*, she thought. *So, I will try hard to love him.* She quietly sat beside the bed and studied his face. It was not an old face, but very thin and white with curls atop his head. Although he was the same age as Aunt Esther, he lacked her color and vibrance.

A nurse came in and he awoke as she touched his hand. "Time for your medicine, Mr. Larson. Try to sit up. You have company."

He turned his face to the side of the bed where Ruth was sitting and met her eyes. "My child," he said and held out his hand. She arose and placed both her hands in his, not knowing what to say. Dick kept repeating, "My child, my child… I would have known you among hundreds of girls. You have your mother's hair and eyes the color of mine. Thank you for coming."

He wanted to know all about her trip and the accident, while holding her hands tightly. Ruth told him all the sputtering and crashing, and how well they were taken care of at the ranch.

"Thank God it wasn't more harmful to you!" he said earnestly. She was surprised how easily she could talk to her father. He just looked at her and occasionally asked a question. The ice was broken between them. He was a stranger to her no longer. "My dear child," he said, "as soon as I am able, I will take care of the expenses of these good people." Then he asked, "Will you come back tomorrow?"

She smiled "Yes, every day; twice if you want me to."

He beamed, "Do I want you to? It will be hard for me to wait to see you again."

A pleasant surprise awaited Ruth upon returning to her father's house. Two letters—one from Aunt Esther and one from Art Collins. She held them tightly between her lips as she crutched her way as fast as possible to her room to read them.

Aunt Esther wrote that the schools were finally closing for the summer, and she would soon be on her way to California to join her. Joe had told Esther all about their experiences and, according to his story, the ranch must have been a wonderful place. He couldn't praise it enough.

Ruth read Art Collins' letter over and over again. He was telling her about little Donna crying when she found the room empty, and her angel gone. "I heard her mother say, 'Donna, stop crying. Your angel will come back.' Now I ask you, will she come back and bring a blessing on this house?" Ruth admitted to herself that she would like very much to go back.

The next day, Ruth told her father the story of little Donna and the angel. He was pleased. "I'd like you to buy her the nicest doll you can find. Have it packed and sent to her. Mrs. Donovan will help you." Ruth was delighted. It was not hard at all to love her father, as good and generous as he was to her. The next day he would be brought home and she would help take care of him. And Aunt Esther was coming. How wonderful! They all were so good to her. She surely was blessed by God.

Ruth was standing on the steps in a white dress, sweet to look at, when her father was brought home. She helped Mrs.

Donovan to make him comfortable and then she devoted all her time to him. She read books to him and he asked many questions about her life. He saw that Esther had done a wonderful job in rearing his beautiful daughter. Ruth had the appearance of her parents but the character of her Aunt Esther. "It was the will of God that she raise Ruth, not I," thought Dick. Then he asked Ruth "You've never had a boyfriend?"

"No, Father," she said as she felt the color rise in her face.

He smiled, "Darling, I don't trust that rancher you told me so much about."

Ruth quickly changed the subject. "Father, it's time for your lunch. I'll see about it," and she left the room.

His face sobered. *Oh, I see. He's captured her heart. I hope he is worthy of having her. I'm afraid I just found her only to lose her again.*

Forgiving Love

A telegram announced the imminent arrival of Aunt Esther. Ruth was filled with joy. How she had missed her aunt's companionship! She felt lost without her wisdom and guidance.

Ruth rode with Jim to the train station to greet her. What a happy reunion it was! No daughter could love her mother more than Ruth loved her Aunt Esther.

"Oh, Auntie, we will share my room together. How wonderful! I have so much to tell you."

"How is your father?" Esther asked.

"He's getting along just fine, and he has been a dear. Aunt Esther, please be good to him," she pleaded.

Esther smiled. "Would you trade him for me?"

The very thought of it brought a frown to Ruth's face. "No! Never! Nobody could take your place in my heart. But don't you see, he has nobody to care for him."

"Yes, Darling, I see."

Dick Larson waited at home with mixed feelings. He was happy for Ruth. But the truth was that he feared his sister-in-law. She had been deservedly harsh and unforgiving toward him in the past, and he had no desire to experience all that again.

What Dick did not know was that Esther had had plenty of time for reflection over the last few weeks. She realized how selfish she had been. She considered herself a Christian; but, oh, if it depended on her judgment, no sinner would get into heaven! They would all go the other way—especially Dick! And because we are all sinners before God, heaven would be an empty place. *How wrong I was! May God forgive me.*

On this day, Esther greeted Dick Larson with a friendly smile, which he noticed at once and for which he was grateful. The first chance he had to talk with Esther alone, he said, "Esther, can you please try to forgive me? I snatched Belinda out of your lives without warning and without so much as a last goodbye."

"Yes, Dick," she answered, "I forgave you before you even asked. I realize I was harsh, and I hope you can forgive me also." He stood up weakly, reached for her hand and kissed it tenderly. "Thank you, Esther. You've made me so happy today. And could I ask one more favor of you?"

"Well, what is it?" she asked.

"I would like for you and Ruth to spend your summer vacation at my home. I would so enjoy your being here. It would be wonderful!"

"I'll think it over, Dick."

"Esther, even if you don't want to stay at my request, you might *need* to stay here to keep an eye on Ruth. If I'm not mistaken, she thinks a lot of that rancher. He's the first man she's ever really gotten acquainted with. We will need to get to know him for the child's sake before it is too late."

"Oh dear!" was all she could say. Yes, she had to stand beside her child. She was an old maid—her whole life revolved around that child—her baby. She asked Dick, "Did you try to get information about him?"

"Yes, I did. The reports are very good. I wrote to him, thanking him for his kindness and asked him to let me know the amount I owed him. I received his answer today. He wrote like a gentleman, saying there was no expense, only pleasure on his part. Would you think it wise to send Mr. Collins an invitation to come here and be our guest at his convenience?"

"Yes, indeed! I would like very much to meet him. He writes to Ruth. She gave me the letters to read. Fine, interesting letters they were."

Art Collins wrote back to accept their invitation with pleasure.

Dick and Aunt Esther decided to keep the plans for his coming a secret from Ruth. Meanwhile, Esther enjoyed listening to Dick's stories of his life and travels, and Dick enjoyed relating them to her. They spent much time together in the garden and took many scenic drives in his car. Esther had never had a vacation where she felt so completely relaxed. She was enjoying every minute.

Chapter Twelve

Enduring Love

Art arrived in Ventura sooner than they expected. He stopped his car in front of Dick Larson's home and did just what every good rancher would have done—sat quietly for a while to get the lay of the land. From where he sat, he could see part of a fine garden and, if he were not mistaken, the glimpse of a white dress peeking through the green bushes.

He left the car to make a beeline for that white dress. Not seeing a gate, he swung himself easily over the fence as lightly as a deer without touching it. As he approached her, his heart began to pound. Ruth was picking oranges, the basket beside her almost full. Her back was turned to him. She was standing on her tiptoes, stretching in vain to reach another orange. He walked on the soft grass, avoiding the gravel walk, so she would not hear his approach. When he reached above her hand to bend the twig down, Ruth gave a startled cry and spun around quickly. Art looked smilingly into her eyes, still holding the branch.

"Surprised?" he asked. She blushed and held out her hand in greeting, but he grasped both of her hands instead. "I am unspeakably happy to see you!" he said. She seemed very pleased, but what he was looking for and hoping to see was not there as he searched her eyes. He would try again. Meanwhile, he would help her fill the basket. Then, talking happily, they slowly walked toward the house.

"Did you drive here?" she asked.

"Yes, and it was the longest trip I ever made. I mean it seemed so long. Your father was very kind to send me an invitation."

"He did?" That was a surprise for Ruth. "Oh! That was nice of him, and now you can meet Aunt Esther. I know you will like her too."

"I'm sure I will."

Esther was looking out of the window and saw them come. She turned to her brother-in-law: "Is this young man with Ruth a friend of yours?"

He stepped to the window and said, "I must say he is a stranger to me."

The surprise was on them when they came in and Ruth introduced Art Collins. He looked more like a well-dressed businessman—not how they expected a rancher to look. Ruth's father greeted his guest heartily. Esther was her own sweet self, and they made him feel right at home. Ruth questioned him about Donna, the dogs, and all the people and things that had captured her heart during the short time she stayed at the ranch. Art gladly answered.

"The little dog I promised you is learning his lessons fast. I picked the smartest one of the bunch and he gets his training every day."

"I hope you do not expect too much from him," Ruth said with concern.

"No, not too bad," he laughed. "After all, he needs to learn how to please his master. Or rather his mistress."

After dinner, while Esther retired to her room for a nap and Dick rested in his chair on the terrace, Art and Ruth walked into the garden. She looked more beautiful to him than ever. He noticed the dimples in her cheeks when she smiled and her graceful movements. He longed to touch her hair but did not dare. She was nearly sacred to him, like a beautiful white rose.

In the morning, Esther arose earlier than the others, for she had not yet adjusted to the three-hour time difference between Michigan and California. She found Mrs. Donovan in the kitchen preparing breakfast and stepped right in to help. The two ladies worked well together. Mrs. Donovan enjoyed having another guest in the house after all these quiet years in Mr. Larson's home. When she could no longer keep her thoughts to herself, she quietly asked Esther the question that had been nagging at her.

"If it's not too bold for me to ask, what are your thoughts on Mr. Art?"

"He seems to be a fine young man, clean and upright. Do you agree?"

Mrs. Donovan smiled. "I do indeed. I think maybe the

Lord had a hand in dropping Ruth down safely at his front door."

For four days, the little group shared many happy hours. Mr. Larson went out of his way to make things pleasant for his guests. He had plenty of time to relax during this period of convalescence and he especially enjoyed the young man's company. Ruth did not mind at all. She was enjoying her time with Aunt Esther, with whom she could share her deepest thoughts and feelings. And she had many new ones to share!

Of course, Art would have liked to take Ruth out alone, but he knew her Aunt Esther would require a chaperone. He completely understood her desire to protect such a treasure. As it was, he was thankful just to be near Ruth and hear her talk and laugh. She was a very special young lady, and her father and aunt were also fine people. He realized that they needed to know more about him… and they had a right to evaluate his character! Indeed, if given the opportunity to win the heart of a pearl like Ruth, he would also watch over her diligently.

When it came time for Art to return home, he obtained Mr. Larson's promise that he would soon bring the two ladies to pay a visit and see his ranch. All three stood on the terrace waving "goodbye." It was a bittersweet parting. As much as Art hated to leave Ruth behind, he rejoiced in knowing that he had found two true friends in Dick and Esther.

Dick's health improved daily. How he enjoyed the company of these two lovely ladies! The thought of losing

them frightened him. His house had become a real home with Ruth singing and laughing as she glided through the rooms. She had completely lost her shyness toward him. Every evening, before she retired to her room, she gave him a big hug and a kiss goodnight. How sweet his daughter was! He hated to think of missing that again. Esther became a real pal. They enjoyed talking about their college days back in their younger years.

Esther was by heart a fine character. Never did she bring up the past. She knew that if one forgives, one also must try to forget. She herself had experienced God's grace, and it was now her turn to pass on His forgiving love to Dick.

One day Dick surprised his daughter and Esther by saying, "Today I feel fine and back to my normal self. What would you think about a trip to Arizona?"

Ruth's eyes sparkled. She didn't say a word but looked toward her aunt to decide. Aunt Esther asked Dick, "Are you sure you can stand the long drive?"

"I really expect you two ladies to help me," he answered.

"There is no need to hurry, so we can take plenty of time and enjoy the scenery in Arizona. It's a very pretty state with its vast expanse of colorful desert, rocky areas and saguaro cactus."

Ruth perked up. "Are those the things that look like tall men with arms sticking up?" Dick nodded. "I wondered what those were! I saw them from the train."

They decided to make it a surprise visit to Art and started out on Monday morning. They were as happy as three children going on a picnic! The trip was thoroughly pleasant

and enjoyable. Dick took them north for a breathtaking view of the Grand Canyon before heading east to the ranch. Driving only for short periods, they arrived on Friday about 5:00 p.m.

Ruth was driving and brought the car slowly to a stop in front of the ranch house. Caro, the German Shepherd, greeted Ruth with happy yelps. "He remembers me!" she said to her aunt. "When I sat in my wheelchair, he would lie beside me on the veranda."

The dog's barking brought Sam to the door. "Mary," he called into the house, "Miss Ruth and her folks are here." Mary came running. She greeted them happily while Sam carried their baggage inside.

Mary led the guests to the living room, explaining Art Collins' absence. "The boss is rounding up steers with the cowhands, driving them to separate pastures to be fattened up for sale. Are you hungry? Or would you rather wait for the boss to come home?"

They decided to wait. It was Esther's first visit to a real ranch home—a comfortable big house with a veranda. Plain but very tastefully furnished. She liked it.

Ruth excused herself to go looking for her little friend, Donna. Mary directed her to the yard beyond the kitchen where she was chattering to the puppies and playing with her new doll. As Ruth stepped out of the house, Donna jumped up, crying, "The angel came back!" The happy little child held out her arms to Ruth and clung tightly, showering her with hugs and kisses.

In the kitchen, Mary was telling her husband Sam, "I surely like Miss Ruth's aunt!" Poor Mr. Larson did not fare so well in Mary's opinion. She decided she didn't care so much for menfolk anyway. He probably was all right, being Miss Ruth's father and all, but he certainly couldn't compare with Ruth and Aunt Esther.

Meanwhile, Ruth and Donna enjoyed their time together by sitting on the swing. Donna was a talkative child, and it didn't take long before Ruth knew everything going on the ranch that was of interest to a little girl. Eventually she led Donna into the living room to meet her father and aunt and gave her all the fine presents she had brought from California. Mary feared that her happy little girl would keep her tired mother awake half the night, unable to sleep after all the excitement.

The sun had long since disappeared before the cowboys rode in, tired and dirty after a hard day's work. Sam had hidden Dick's car in the garage. After caring for their horses, the men walked to the big watering trough where, with a lot of splashing, they washed their hands and faces, heads, and necks while their guests watched slyly through the windows. *How cooling and refreshing that water must feel!* Ruth thought. Then the men piled happily into the kitchen where a long table was set for a good supper. Art's three guests were still hiding in the living room.

Sam informed him, "Your dinner is waiting in the dining room, Mr. Art."

"All right, Sam, I'm good and hungry tonight," he replied.

"But I'd rather not eat alone!" As he opened the dining room door, he asked in surprise, "Table set for four?"

"Yes, company arrived late this afternoon." A few long strides brought him to the living room door. He expected to see the neighbors who often dropped in unexpectedly. What a surprise! He only had eyes for Ruth and strode quickly toward her, taking both her hands in his and looking lovingly into her shining eyes. Saying not a word, he touched her silky hair and stammered, "Ruth." They seemed to forget the presence of others in the room. For the first time, Art saw the love in her eyes that made them shine like stars. He whispered again and again, "My angel." For a long moment, all was quiet. Then Sam broke the silence by appearing in the door.

"Dinner is served!"

Art turned toward his voice, still holding Ruth's hands. Then Dick approached Art to shake his hand and Esther offered a gentle hug.

Art found his voice. "I'm unspeakably happy to see you! I'm sorry I wasn't here to greet you when you arrived."

Dick Larson laughed, "Plenty of time for that. We would not have known to tell you what time we would arrive anyway, as we wanted to enjoy our leisurely trip."

A delicious, wholesome dinner was served by Mary. Art sat across the table from Ruth. As hungry as he was, he spent more time feasting his eyes on Ruth than eating his dinner. He was happily unaware of the fact that he hadn't even changed out of his dirty clothes before dinner or he would

have felt self-conscious. But he was completely engrossed with the fact that his beloved was sitting at his table.

What a wonderful ending to a hard, tiresome day! The four spent the rest of the warm evening visiting on the veranda with Caro lying beside Ruth. Oh, how Art wanted to caress her, to stroke her shining hair and to touch those sweet cheeks!

The next day Art invited his guests to see the ranch and the cattle. He drove them to all the places he could reach with his car and they returned home hours later with the best of appetites. Mary was in her glory when everybody enjoyed her good cooking. Dick felt the influence of outdoor life already, resulting in a healthy appetite and a good night's sleep. There was no need for sleeping pills in this place!

One beautiful night later, Ruth asked shyly of Art, "Would you ask the boys to sing and play as they did before? I know Auntie and Father would love it." He was happy to do her that favor and walked over to the bunkhouse to get the boys together.

Red, the Foreman, was ready to go. "Come on, boys, we sure can do it." Before long they were standing around the veranda, playing and singing.

Ruth leaned toward Art so he could hear her better and said, "There's an especially good tenor voice missing. Where is he?"

Art's face turned red, and Ruth knew at once that the missing tenor she had heard so distinctly that evening was Art's. Mischief twinkled in her eyes as she asked, "Won't you

please replace the missing link?" He immediately joined the singers, and Ruth couldn't hold back her smile as she listened to his beautiful tenor voice. How happy she was to realize that it was he who had sung under her window! That kind of serenading was something she had only read about in fairy tales. Now it was *her* story!

Father and Aunt Esther also enjoyed the singing and playing. As the darkness settled in, Art invited the boys into the living room where Ruth played the piano and everyone joined in the singing. Mary served delicious sandwiches which disappeared rapidly. The boys had enormous appetites and could devour mountains of food. The time passed too quickly for all of them. When each one retired to their respective rooms, the ranch lay very quiet, with only the occasional bark of a dog.

At the breakfast table, Art asked, "Would you all like to go out riding today?" He wanted to devote his time to his guests.

"I never in my life was on a horse's back," Aunt Esther smiled. "And I'd like to keep it that way."

Dick Larson also declined the invitation, as horseback riding would be much too strenuous for him in his present condition.

Ruth's eyes sparkled. "I would like to try it! In fact, I brought a riding outfit along, a present from my father." She hurried to the guestroom to change into the riding habit. Then she rushed outside to find Art waiting with the horses.

He grinned at her. "You look adorable." He lifted Ruth

into the saddle and smiled up at her. "This horse is especially trained for you, faithful and quiet."

"I'm not afraid as long as you are here. And I hope someday to become a very good rider." Then she looked away from him toward Aunt Esther, who was standing on the steps with her father, warning them to be very careful.

Art walked to her and said, "Miss Esther, I'll take mighty good care of Miss Ruth," and he leaned down to whisper into her ear. "If need be, I'd lay my life down for her and you know it, don't you?"

She looked into his sincere eyes and answered, "Yes, Art, I do."

The horses were fidgeting, eager to get moving. Art mounted his horse while young Pete held the reins of Ruth's horse. He handed them to Ruth, stepped aside, and the two rode off.

Pete turned to Aunt Esther and said, "Well, the boss is blind as far as we're concerned. He only has eyes for Ruth. Never saw him like that before!"

"No," Bill said thoughtfully, "don't know as I blame him. She's a mighty fine girl. I guess it will be up to us to keep the ranch going for a spell while he's courting. Let's saddle up and go. Yippee-hi-yah!"

Dick and Esther remained on the veranda for a while, side by side, watching Ruth and Art ride away. When Dick finally turned to speak to Esther, tears were streaming down her cheeks. He tenderly laid his arm around her shoulders.

"Please don't cry, Esther. You will always have Ruth's

deepest love and respect, and Art's as well. Instead of one child, you will have two children who love you!"

Esther turned and looked thoughtfully into his eyes. "You've changed, Dick. Please forgive me for saying this but, in the past, it seems you thought only about your own happiness. But it seems your heart has softened toward others. How did that happen?"

"Yes, Esther. I am different. When I faced the prospect of dying alone as an empty, miserable man with no hope and no future, I remembered how joyful you and Belinda were when you talked about your God. I decided to call Belinda's pastor. My heart was finally open enough to grasp the truth each time he came and instructed me in the faith. Eventually I understood that our Heavenly Father loved me so much that He sent His only-begotten Son, Jesus, to take on our human flesh and unite Himself to man, to me, so that I could be filled with the Holy Spirit and united to God! He saved me from my self-centered way of life and filled me with His peace and joy. I was baptized into His family forever. Never again will I be empty and alone. I feel like a new person, Esther, and I think Belinda would be very happy about it."

Esther nodded as a tear slipped down her cheek. "I'm sure she is thrilled, Dick! The Bible says we're surrounded by a great cloud of witnesses cheering us on! I like to think Belinda and Mama are part of that group, celebrating your new life."

Dick nodded. "Me too. Especially now that I'm a believer like our dear daughter Ruth… and you." He gave

her a sideways look and she saw both the sparkle and the question in his eyes. "We're all united in God's family now. Would you mind, Esther, sharing your family with me too?"

Esther gripped his arm and moved next to him. "We've come full circle, haven't we, Dick? It's not the love story I had imagined, but I think it's even better! We are family indeed and I think we will soon be sharing the pitter patter of little feet."

As they turned to watch Ruth and Art ride out of sight, Dick silently slid his hand over Ether's and grinned.

S. **Stories** create a memorable way of learning new ideas through someone else's experience.

Q. **Questions** lead us to wrestle with new ideas and process what they really mean.

J. **Journaling** helps us imagine how those ideas might look in our own lives.

S.Q.J. is the secret ingredient that propels learning from Informational to Transformational!

Questions for Small Group Discussion
and Journaling for Personal Growth

Chapter 1 Blooming Love

1. As an only child, Dick envied larger families where the children had others to argue with and share their troubles. Did you ever wish you had more or fewer siblings? What are the benefits of a small family versus a large family?

2. Esther is a sincere Christian with no experience in dating. Although Dick has no religious upbringing or interest in Christ, he visits Esther's church so he can ask her out on a date, knowing where to find her on a Sunday. Do you think they would have made a good

match? How important do you think it is for a spouse to share your same spiritual beliefs?

3.   Blooming love often involves anticipation, wonder, and infatuation. How have you experienced blooming love in your own life story? How did it impact your life?

Chapter 2 Selfish Love

1.   Dick was speechless when he first saw Belinda. He thought she was the most beautiful girl he had ever seen. Do you believe in love at first sight? Why or why not?

2.   Belinda thinks her sister takes life too seriously, always studying and planning for the future. Esther thinks Belinda takes life too lightly, thus she feels responsible for Belinda and concerned that her heart might get broken. Yet Belinda doesn't seem to care about Esther's heart!

     How would you have felt in Esther's shoes? How could Dick and Belinda have handled the situation better in order to protect everyone's hearts?

3.   Selfish love involves thinking only about one's own needs and desires without caring about the needs and desires of the other. Have you ever been in a one-way relationship where one person cares more than the

other? How did that make you feel? How did it impact your life?

Chapter 3 Healing Love

1. After Belinda disappears, Esther feels responsible to care for their aging mother. Have you ever been a caregiver for a loved one? How did you handle the loneliness? Were you envious of friends who had more freedom? If you don't have personal experience with this, can you share about a friend or relative in a similar situation?

2. Esther is amazed at how quickly her mother was able to forgive Belinda for eloping. She was also relieved that her mother didn't blame her for letting it happen. Esther felt a great burden lift when she and her mother were able to let go of the shock, forgive Belinda, hoping for her marriage to be blessed, and then enjoy their own times together. Do you think you could have forgiven Belinda so easily? When hurt by someone you love, are you able to embrace the ones who do love you well and refocus your love in positive ways?

3. Healing love often involves forgiving the one who wronged you and embracing those who can love you well. How have you experienced healing love in your life?

4. Challenge: Is there someone in your life story whom you need to forgive? Might you say a prayer, write a letter, or make a phone call in order to set yourself free from any bitterness you might be holding in your heart?

Chapter 4 Love Letters

1. Esther and her mother eagerly awaited every little scrap of news from Belinda and cherished her letters when they arrived, especially the news of a baby on the way. In today's world of texts and emails, how do you feel when you receive a handwritten letter? Do you send them?

2. Esther was content with her simple lifestyle. She discovered that contentment is not found in getting what you want but wanting what you get. She wasn't like other young girls her age who "were never satisfied and wore themselves out grabbing for things they couldn't reach." Why do you think it's easy nowadays to become materialistic and discontent? Have you ever struggled to feel content in your situation?

3   Love letters often involve words that express love or create feelings of love in our own hearts. Have you ever received or sent a love letter? How did it affect your heart?

Chapter 5 Courageous Love

1. Dick blamed the baby for Belinda's death and didn't even want to see her, let alone be her dad. In contrast, Esther found a new life purpose in loving the tiny infant. How do you think Esther's faith or Dick's lack of faith affected their differing responses to the same tragedy?

2. Esther had a lot to learn about taking care of a newborn. The cross-country train ride was probably more challenging than the narrative lets on. What do you think is the most difficult adjustment when a new baby comes into your life? If you raised children of your own, did your parenting style change as you grew more experienced?

3. Courageous love involves putting aside our own comfort in order to save or protect another. Have you experienced someone doing that for you? Have you ever exercised courageous love on behalf of another?

Chapter 6 Motherly Love

1. Ruth was only three years old when her beloved grandmother died. How old were you when you first lost a loved one? How did that affect your family, especially during holidays, birthdays, or anniversaries? What did you do to keep that person "alive" in your heart and mind?

2. Ruth was afraid of thunderstorms and thought it was "God bowling in heaven." What motherly skills did Esther use to comfort her? What were you afraid of when you were a child? What helped you overcome your fears?

3. Motherly love involves nurturing and tending to needs, comforting, feeding, nursing, as well as teaching life principles and skills. Was your mother able to do those things well for you? If you are a mother, what does motherly love feel like or compel you to do? Did it come naturally to you or was it a struggle?

4. Challenge: When Dick suddenly shows up and wants to be a part of Ruth's life, Esther feels threatened and resists. In church, she hopes Dick is listening to the sermon so he can think about his wrongdoings and repent. By focusing on him, she is blinded to her own sins—her critical, judgmental attitude and lack of understanding how people can make bad decisions when overcome with grief. Is there someone in your life whom you find easy to criticize, question their motives, or judge their actions? What things in their past might be causing them to act this way? What things in your past might "push your buttons" or cause you to over-react where this person is concerned?

Chapter 7 Love Letting Go

1. Now that Ruth is a senior in high school, Esther allows her to make her own decision about visiting her father. How old were you when your parents started letting you make your own decisions? Did they prepare you well to make wise choices? Are there any decisions you regret?

2. Ruth chose to go visit her father so she wouldn't feel guilty if he died. Although her motives were more selfish rather than out of concern for her father's well-being, it seemed like the right decision. Have you ever decided something out of a wrong motive but later, your heart changed, and the circumstances caused you to grow in ways you didn't expect?

3. Letting go is perhaps one of the most difficult aspects of parenting. Did your parents do a good job of letting you spread your wings? Have you struggled with letting your own children go when they came of age? Can you give an example?

Chapter 8 A Child's Love

1. Echoing what happened when Dick first met Belinda, Art was struck eighteen years later by Ruth's breathtaking beauty. However, unlike Dick, Art treated Ruth with the utmost of respect and did not act on

his feelings while Ruth was in a vulnerable situation. Describe several ways in which Dick's and Art's actions differed.

2. Little Donna is quite taken with Ruth and thinks she's an angel that God brought to their ranch. Despite how weak Ruth was feeling, she took time to play with Donna, making doll clothes and sharing stories. Donna's mother was too busy working to play with her daughter in the same way. Was there someone in your childhood, or even now as an adult, who was like a favorite aunt or mother-figure to you? How did that person make a difference in your life?

3. A child's love can feel so sweet and innocent when they snuggle next to you and look up into your eyes. How have you experienced a child's love in your life? Can you imagine ever looking up at God that way?

Chapter 9 A Gentleman's Love

1. Art found himself falling in love with Ruth and believed that God brought her into his life because she was meant for him. Do you believe that God has a chosen person for each of us that is His perfect will, or do you think love is left up to chance or our own decisions? Explain your answer.

2. When Ruth leaves for California, she and Art promise to correspond and continue their friendship by mail. Do you think the days before FaceTime, email, and texting were more romantic with handwritten letters and perhaps poems written to a loved one? Or do you think that long-distance relationships would have been harder to maintain?

3. A gentleman's love involves thoughtfulness and respect, in contrast to selfishness and lust. Have you ever experienced a gentleman's love? If so, who was the gentleman and how did you feel being around him?

Chapter 10 Father Love

1. At first Ruth felt awkward around Dick and tried to love him simply because he was her father, but as time went on, she genuinely enjoyed his company. She recognized that generosity was his way of showing his love for her, offering to pay for all her expenses during recuperation and giving her money to buy a beautiful doll for Donna. It's often easier for people, especially men of Dick's generation, to show love through giving gifts, helping with a project, or fixing something, rather than by saying the words, "I love you." When you were a child, how did your family show their love for you? Does your family express love differently today?

2. As Dick learns more about his daughter's life and experiences, he believes it was better for Ruth to have been raised by Esther rather than by him. He sees in Ruth the godly character of her aunt and grandmother. How do you think Ruth's life would have been different had she been raised in wealth and affluence by a single father who had no belief in God?

3. Fatherly love involves protecting and providing for his child. Did you have a father who was able to do that for you well? Have you experienced that kind of love with your Heavenly Father?

Chapter 11 Forgiving Love

1. Dick was nervous about meeting Esther again because she was harsh and unforgiving in their last encounter. When he asks forgiveness for snatching Belinda away without a goodbye, Esther not only forgives him but apologizes in return for being harsh. Their beautiful reconciliation may never have happened if Dick had not grown ill and needed a life-threatening surgery! Has there been a time in your life where God used a negative circumstance to cause something good to happen? Share your experience.

2. After Esther forgives Dick deeply from her heart, she is able to thoroughly enjoy her time in California and

feels she has never had such a refreshing vacation. Have you ever been in a similar situation where you were able to let go of an offense and feel the burden lifted from your shoulders, letting you enjoy life in a new way?

3. Forgiving love does not deny that an offense has occurred. Rather, it releases the offender into the hands of God and sets ourselves free to let go of the pain. How have you experienced forgiving love in your life? Were you the receiver or the giver of forgiveness?

Chapter 12 Enduring Love

1. Art wanted time alone with Ruth but chose to respect her parents' wishes to protect her with a chaperone. Instead of dating, they spent their time together with her family. The result was that Dick and Esther quickly accepted him and trusted him more fully than if he had taken Ruth away on dates alone. What do you think about the old-fashioned way of courting compared to the casual dating practices of today? Do you think our society could benefit by learning from the past? Explain your rationale.

2. Dick shared with Esther how his illness caused him to think about where he might spend eternity if he died, which led him to contact Belinda's pastor. This

is the first time in the story where we learn that Belinda went to church alone after they were married. Although she wrote in her letters that she was very happy, Belinda didn't choose to share this part of her life with her family. Why do you think she withheld that information? Do you think Belinda might have regretted quickly marrying someone whose faith and values did not match her own? Why or why not?

3. Enduring love involves a strength that can withstand the ups and downs of life and remain united. We live in a fallen world and, since nobody is perfect, intimate relationships will always require humility and forgiveness along with the sweetness of romantic love. Do you agree? How have you experienced enduring love in your life?

About the Author

Constance Menzel Manthei was born in Wotostwo, Province Posen in the German Empire (Now Poland). She experienced six years of tender love and care before her mother tragically died in childbirth. For the next eight years, like Cinderella, she endured torture at the hands of a hateful stepmother until her father left that wife and took the children to his hometown of Freiberg, Silesia. Constance delighted in the lush landscape and jolly folk of Silesia while finishing school and learning domestic skills.

Constance immigrated to America in 1900 and married Ferdinand Manthei, who had also immigrated from Wotostwo. The young couple settled in Petoskey, Michigan, and bought a small farm. Despite years of poverty in a difficult marriage, Constance sprinkled many shades of love into the lives of her children and grandchildren. She taught them the Christian faith and the value of hard work, healthy food, friendship, music, and a great sense of humor. A great storyteller, Constance experienced shades of love which she then wove into her own version of a romance novel.

Constance recapped her life journey saying, "I was led up and down but always protected by the Lord," illustrating the truth that "God is able to work all things together for good to those who love Him."

Family Comments

"Constance Menzel Manthei (1884-1952), also remembered in German as Grossmama Konstanze, wrote this story sometime before 1951. She wrote her life story first, then this story. She got her ideas while sleeping."

Christel Manthei Cone,
Daughter of Constance Manthei
March 12, 2003

"Grossmama was a real romantic. I did not know this side of her."

Darwin Gene Cone
Grandson of Constance Manthei
March 12, 2003

"Not your formula romance! This story deepened my capacity to see life through the many shades of love. Although Grandma Constance wrote this ages ago, the story is timeless... and worth sharing!"

Ruth Manthei Wilkey
Granddaughter and Editor